Why Coyote Sings to the Moon
author Ellen Jackson
illustrated by Eric Joyner

Text copyright © 1995 by author
Illustrations copyright © 1995 by Eric Joyner
Designed by Russ Maselli

Published in 1995 by American Editions
150 East Wilson Bridge Road
Suite 145 Columbus, Ohio, 43085, USA

American Editions is an imprint of American Education Publishing Co.

ISBN 1-56189-398-6
Printed in the United States of America

WHY COYOTE SINGS to the MOON

Ellen Jackson ● Illustrated by Eric Joyner
American Editions ● Columbus ● Ohio

In the days when the earth was young, the Creator decided to make a new kind of animal. First he scooped up a handful of clay and formed the beginning of a head. Then he cut a slash for the mouth. Before he could go any further, the mouth began to jabber.

"Could you make the eyes next? And my ears should be big and pointed. I want to be able to hear and see a mouse on a dark night, so give me the best of everything."

The Creator wasn't used to being ordered around, but he liked this bold new creature, so he did as he was told.

"Can you make my legs strong for chasing rabbits? And my coat of fur should be soft and silky," said Coyote, for that was the new animal's name.

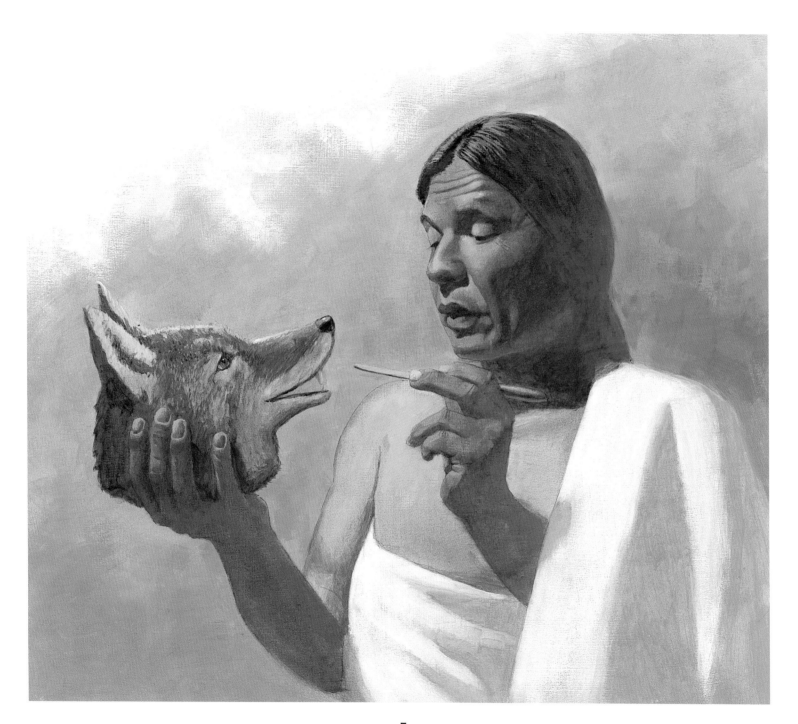

The Creator gave Coyote the best of everything just as he had asked. Then he handed Coyote a mirror so that he could admire himself.

"Good work," said Coyote. "Oh! One more thing. I'd like wings so that I could fly around that big silver ball up there and see what's on the other side."

"That silver ball is the moon," said the Creator. "I can't give you wings. Your place is here on earth. But because I like you so much, I'm going to give you four lives."

Coyote was very pleased. He trotted off to tell all the other animals about his good fortune.

"How many lives did you get?" he asked Turtle.

"I'll bet you didn't get four lives," he bragged to Lizard.

Then he started thinking.

"Four lives are fine, but it would surely be exciting to fly around the moon and see the other side. Now that would be something!"

Coyote sighed. He looked for the moon, but it was hidden behind a cloud. He climbed to the top of a mountain and looked across the carpet of clouds that now stretched beneath him. There he saw the moon rising in the sky.

"I know," thought Coyote, "I'll walk across those gray fluffy things. They'll take me right to the moon."

He leaped into the air toward the closest cloud. SWOOSH! Down, down through the cloud Coyote fell.

For three winters Coyote lay flattened against the earth. Then he finally managed to pull himself together. Soon he was his old self, bragging and carrying on as if nothing had happened.

"I was close," he told Raccoon. "I almost made it to the moon!"

When the Creator looked down and saw how Coyote was behaving, he decided to pay him a visit.

"Coyote," said the Creator. "This won't do. You've used up one life already. You belong here on earth like the other animals. Coyotes were not meant to visit the moon."

"But ..." said Coyote.

"That's final!" said the Creator and he wrapped himself in a bright cloud and vanished.

Coyote had another idea. He struck up a friendship with two eagles.

"I, myself, am a traveler, you know," said Coyote. "Not so long ago, I almost walked to the moon. I'm getting ready to go again soon to see the other side. Why don't you come along?"

"Oh, I don't see how we could go," one eagle said.

"We know the air routes, but we're not much good on the ground," his mate agreed.

"That's not a problem," said Coyote, putting his plan into action. "We'll go by wing this time."

So the eagles grabbed hold of Coyote with their talons. Then they beat their wings and beat their wings until they all rose up into the night sky.

But the moon was nowhere in sight.

"I know I saw it over there," said one of the eagles, nodding toward a nearby cliff. "Just last week, in fact. Let's head in that direction."

"No, no, my dear," said his mate, pointing the other way. "You're wrong. The moon was on the other side of the ridge last week."

"It was in the east," the other insisted.

"No, sweet'ums, it was in the west," said his mate firmly.

"East!" said the first eagle, waving a talon in one direction.

"West!" cried the other, waving a talon in the opposite direction.

As they argued, both eagles let go of poor Coyote. Down, down he tumbled.

This time Coyote had fallen from a great height. For four winters Coyote lay in pieces across the landscape. Then one morning his right leg woke up.

"Yoohoo! Where is everyone?" asked the leg.

"I'm over here," said the head.

Little by little, all the pieces of Coyote came back together. Coyote found his ears under a bush and his tail dangling from the branch of a tree.

Again the Creator came to see him. "I told you before, Coyote, your place is here on earth," said the Creator. "You have only two lives left. You must stop this foolishness at once," and, with a flash, the Creator disappeared.

But Coyote still longed to see the other side of the moon. One night, he looked up and saw a shining comet with a tail that stretched across the sky.

"Maybe I could ride on that comet," he thought. "I wonder if anyone has ever done that."

"Oh Comet!" called Coyote in his loudest voice. "Could I ride on you?"

"Come up to the mountain and grab onto my tail," said the comet.

So Coyote went up to the top of the mountain and grabbed onto the comet's tail. WHOOSH! Up they went.

Around and around they flew, Coyote and the comet. They zoomed here and they zoomed there.

"Oh Comet," said Coyote. "This is wonderful fun. But it would really be exciting if you would take me on a quick trip around the moon. I've always wanted to see the other side."

"Why not?" said the comet.

"I'm going to see the other side of the moon! Oh, I'm surely the most amazing animal that ever was!" cried Coyote with delight.

The comet zoomed toward the full moon.

"Go slower!" shrieked Coyote as they zipped behind the moon. "I can't see a thing."

The back side of the moon was as dark as a bear's nose at midnight.

In a moment, they were roaring back toward earth. Then, suddenly, Coyote lost his grip and, like a meteor, he fell. Down, down, down he went. SPLAT!

This time Coyote was smashed into a fine powder. Five winters passed before he could pull himself together. Finally, he was his old self again, more or less. Once more the Creator came down to talk to Coyote.

"Now you only have one life left like everyone else," said the Creator. "Why wouldn't you listen to me?"

"The moon is so beautiful," said Coyote, hanging his head. "I just couldn't help being foolish."

The Creator sighed.

"I, too, love beauty. The earth and all its creatures are dear to me, including you, Coyote, in spite of your foolishness. So I'll give you one last gift—a special song to sing to the silver moon."

And so it was. If you listen very carefully on moonlit nights, you can hear Coyote sing his moonsong still.